# Who Has the
## in Class

D1503679

OTHER YEARLING BOOKS YOU WILL ENJOY:

THE SMALL POTATOES CLUB, *Harriet Ziefert*

THE SMALL POTATOES AND THE MAGIC SHOW,
*Harriet Ziefert* and *Jon Ziefert*

THE SMALL POTATOES AND THE BIRTHDAY PARTY,
*Harriet Ziefert* and *Jon Ziefert*

THE SMALL POTATOES AND THE SLEEP-OVER,
*Harriet Ziefert* and *Jon Ziefert*

RAMONA THE BRAVE, *Beverly Cleary*

RAMONA THE PEST, *Beverly Cleary*

RAMONA QUIMBY, AGE 8, *Beverly Cleary*

THE BEAST IN MS. ROONEY'S ROOM, *Patricia Reilly Giff*

FISH FACE, *Patricia Reilly Giff*

IN THE DINOSAUR'S PAW, *Patricia Reilly Giff*

YEARLING BOOKS are designed especially to entertain and enlighten young people. Charles F. Reasoner, Professor Emeritus of Children's Literature and Reading, New York University, is consultant to this series.

For a complete listing of all Yearling titles, write to Dell Publishing Co., Inc., Promotion Department, P.O. Box 3000, Pine Brook, N.J. 07058.

# Who Has
# the Lucky-Duck
# in Class 4-B?

Maggie Twohill

A YEARLING BOOK

Published by
Dell Publishing Co., Inc.
1 Dag Hammarskjold Plaza
New York, New York 10017

Yearling ® TM 913705, Dell Publishing Co., Inc.

ISBN: 0-440-49533-4

Reprinted by arrangement with Bradbury Press, an affiliate of
Macmillan, Inc.
Printed in the United States of America
January 1986

10 9 8 7 6 5 4 3 2 1

CW

This is for the children at
The Windward School
*Thomas J. Bamrick, Director*

# Contents

# Who Has the Lucky-Duck in Class 4-B?

# 1
## Spelling Bee

Elfrida Rapp glanced out the window at the playground. She squirmed in her seat. It was going to be a warm spring. She had worn a sweater to school and knew she wouldn't need it at recess. She straightened the books on her desk and cupped her chin in her hand. Her classmates had begun to talk and whisper.

"Where did Mrs. Berry go?" Tommy Lundgren asked, leaning toward Elfrida.

Elfrida shrugged. "To the john, I guess," she answered. "I don't know."

"She always goes to the john between subjects," Tommy sighed. The class had just finished science.

"She likes to fix her makeup," Carrie List said, turning around. "She puts on new lipstick all the time. She wears it away with all the talking she does."

"Well, it gives us a break," Tommy said. "She can put lipstick on all she wants."

"She does her hair, too," Carrie added.

Elfrida picked up her spelling book and turned to the week's lesson. She stared at each word for a moment, then closed her eyes and spelled to herself, mouthing the letters.

"Aw, you know them already, Elf," Carrie said, watching her. "You always do."

"Are we going to have a spelling bee today?" Ralph Buck asked out loud.

"We have a spelling bee *every* Friday," Melissa Brabble answered. "You know that, Ralph. We *always* have one. And I hope you're not on *my* team."

"I hope I'm not, too," Ralph grumbled.

Carrie turned to Elfrida. "What're you doing for your science project, Elf?" she asked.

"I'm not sure. What are you doing?"

Carrie rubbed a fingernail across her lips. "Maybe something with flowers," she answered. "I like flowers. And they're all around now since the weather's been so nice."

"Flowers is a good idea," Elfrida said. "Maybe I'll do something with the pictures I've been taking of those plants we started from seeds."

"Mine never grew," Carrie said.

"Only I'll bet everybody does a project like that," Elfrida went on, "since we all started plants and we all took pictures of them."

Tommy looked at his watch. "Boy, Mrs. Berry ought to look like a movie star by now!" he said. At that moment the teacher came back. The class burst into laughter.

Mrs. Berry blushed. She tucked a brown curl behind her ear.

"Thank you, Thomas," she said, and the class laughed again.

"*I* think you look very pretty, Mrs. Berry," Melissa said loudly. Ralph glared at her. "Well, I *do*," Melissa told him.

"Are we ready for a spelling bee?" Mrs. Berry asked, tapping her desk with a pencil.

Everyone but Ralph answered, "Yes, Mrs. Berry!"

"Good, then we'll choose teams. Let's see . . ." She looked over the class. "Why don't you be a captain, Victoria, and . . ."

Ralph ducked as he felt the teacher's glance on him.

". . . Ralph. You be the other captain."

Ralph sighed and slowly stood, while Victoria Hansen moved quickly toward the windows.

"Should I pick first, Mrs. Berry?" Victoria asked. The teacher nodded.

"Elfrida!" Victoria said with a grin.

Elfrida took her place next to her captain.

"Tom," Ralph mumbled from the opposite side of the room, next to the blackboard.

"What?" Mrs. Berry asked, tilting her head. "We didn't hear you, Ralph."

"Tommy!" Ralph bellowed. Then he coughed, swallowed and repeated "Tommy" in a normal-sounding voice.

Tommy Lundgren bounced out of his seat and stood next to Ralph.

The selection went on until all of Class 4-B was standing. Mrs. Berry frowned.

"I'm not sure these teams are very even, class," she said. "The children who always seem to score one hundred are all on Victoria's team."

"We got all the dummies," Tommy whispered to Ralph.

"We do not. *You're* good," Ralph answered back.

"I'm the only one," Tommy said. "Why did you pick Horsejaw?" He nodded his head down the row at a boy named Horslick, whose father was a dentist.

"I *had* to, he was the last one left. Besides, I didn't want to be the only one on my team who doesn't know the words."

"Well, you got your wish . . . What a team!" Tommy looked at the teacher. "Oh, boy, she's getting ready to even things out a little. She's chewing off all that lipstick she just put on."

"Why does she do that, anyway?" Ralph whispered. "She's already old and married with kids! Who's she showing off for?"

"Me," Tommy answered. Ralph rolled his eyes.

"I think . . ." Mrs. Berry said, "that we'll have Fred Horslick change places with Carrie List . . ."

"*Awwwwwww!*" the girls on Victoria's team groaned as Carrie crossed the room.

"And . . . Bradley Morris, you change places with Melissa . . ."

There was another groan, but it was only Melissa's.

"Terrific," Ralph muttered. "Brabble's on my team. Just what I need."

"She's a good speller," Tommy said.

"Yeah, that's one of the reasons I hate her."

Mrs. Berry made several more changes while Class 4-B shuffled its feet, giggled and whispered.

"Fine. Now we're ready," Mrs. Berry said and stood in front of her desk. "Victoria, you chose first, so Ralph will take the first word."

Ralph whimpered slightly but only Tommy heard.

"Squirrel!" Mrs. Berry said firmly.

"Squirrel," Ralph repeated. "Uh, squirrel." Melissa stepped forward from the line and looked at Ralph expectantly. "Squirrel," Ralph said again. Melissa made a face and stepped back in line. "s-q-u . . . Um . . . s-q-u . . . e-r-r-l," Ralph finished. Melissa moaned.

"Victoria?" Mrs. Berry said.

Victoria caught her upper lip between her teeth and whispered "squirrel" to herself. Then, almost without thinking, she reached into the pocket of her smock and closed her fingers around the small object inside. It was her Lucky-Duck, her own special "charm."

6

Squeezing it tightly, she smiled at the teacher and said, "S-Q-U-I-R-R-E-L," and Ralph yelled, "Right! Right! I knew that was it!"

Melissa said, "Well, if you knew it, why didn't you—"

"Don't say it, Melissa," Tommy interrupted.

Mrs. Berry glared at them. "Balloon," she said, turning to Fred Horslick.

By the end of the period, Ralph's team had lost by fourteen points. Victoria's team had all won gold stars.

Mrs. Berry closed her spelling book, told the class to review yesterday's math homework and left the room.

"We should have kept Horsejaw," Ralph said as he and Tommy started for their seats. "He got every word right."

"I'm going to learn how to use makeup like Mrs. Berry," Carrie said to Elfrida when they had returned to their seats. "All that shiny green stuff on her eyelids and those long, long eyelashes . . . It *is* just like a movie star's . . ."

"Yeah, except we're not in the movies. We're

just in 4-B math," Elfrida said. "At least we will be when she gets back . . ."

"I still like it," Carrie said. "And you know what she does with her blusher? She doesn't only put it on her cheeks, she—"

"She puts it on her chin and her nose," Victoria interrupted with a giggle. "I've seen her do it. She's got a mirror in her closet in the back."

"I know!" Carrie cried. "Her blusher's in this little compact and it comes with this nice soft puffy brush . . ."

"My mother uses a cream," Victoria said. "Her fingers are always red with it. A brush is better."

"I personally prefer—" Elfrida began and stretched her arms, yawning, "a sunburn. It's much better. Your cheeks get red and you don't have to carry around a little compact!"

"Well, I get freckles and peel," Carrie told her. "I'll take the compact. You want to come to my house after school today?"

"Okay," Elfrida said, "but I have to go home and walk Risky first. My mom's at work . . ."

"Want to come, Victoria?" Carrie asked.

"Oh . . . I'd like to, but I've got a list of stuff to get for my mother."

"Anything interesting, like cosmetics?" Carrie asked.

Victoria made a face. "No. *She* gets the cosmetics. *I* get the milk of magnesia."

"I know what," Carrie said. "Let's go with Victoria. Let's go shopping first. Then we can go walk Risky together and either stay at your house or go to mine." Carrie loved to go shopping. It never mattered what for.

"Good," Victoria said. "I'd much rather do this stuff with you than by myself."

Mrs. Berry came back into the room at last and began to draw circles on the board and then lines through the circles.

"Oh," Carrie sighed. "I guess we're cutting pies again. I wish we could have another spelling bee instead."

Melissa waved her hand frantically. "Can I put the homework on the board, Mrs. Berry? Can I?"

Mrs. Berry said, "*May* I."

Ralph tried not to smile.

# 2
*Pretending*

"I love grocery stores," Carrie said as the three girls walked into Wakefield Co-op. "I like the smells. And I pretend I'm a housewife planning meals for my family."

"Carrie," Elfrida said, "you could pretend if you were locked up in a room with no windows and no doors!"

Carrie grinned and nodded.

"Why don't you pretend you're a house*husband*," Elfrida suggested. "Men can plan meals, too, you know . . ."

"I can't pretend to be a *man*," Carrie said firmly. "That's a yucky pretend."

Elfrida laughed. "Well, we finally found something you can't pretend!"

"I'd *never* want to be a boy," Victoria said.

"You can't even talk to them. Where's the salad dressing?"

"I think it would be fun to be a boy," Elfrida said, as Victoria poked around the shelves.

*"Why?"*

Elfrida shrugged. "I don't know," she said. "Just to see the difference, I guess."

"The difference is that the only thing they like is sports and they *hate* 'pretends' and when they're not being mean to girls they ignore us."

Victoria mumbled, "American cheese . . ." and went to the dairy counter.

"There are girls who like sports," Elfrida said. "And *we* ignore boys . . . And girls can be mean to them, too."

"Like Melissa?" Carrie asked.

"What about Melissa?" Victoria asked.

"She's mean to boys. Especially Ralph."

"That's because they grew up together," Victoria said. "And besides, Melissa is mean to everybody. All I need now is Brillo and then we can go."

"Where next?"

"The drugstore," Victoria answered.

11

"Oh, I *love* the drugstore!" Carrie cried. Elfrida rolled her eyes.

They left the grocery and headed down Main Street toward the corner drugstore.

"Why do you suppose Melissa is so mean?" Carrie asked.

"She was born that way," Victoria said. "We once had a cat that was born mean, too. It scratched everybody."

"I don't think people are born mean," Elfrida said.

"Oh, yes," Victoria said. "You inherit it. I think from your grandmother. Maybe your *great*-grandmother. I'm not sure. And mean boys get it from their grandfathers."

"Where did you hear that?" Carrie asked.

"I don't remember," Victoria said. "But it's true. And once you're born mean you never change. You stay mean all your life. But you can have nice children."

Elfrida laughed. "But your *grandchildren* could be mean, then, right?"

"Right," Victoria answered. "Here's the drugstore." The door was wide open and they walked in.

"Scrooge changed," Elfrida said. "In *A*

*Christmas Carol*. Remember? He was mean and then he turned nice at the end."

"Yeah, but that was only a story," Victoria said. "If three ghosts walked in on Melissa, she could turn nice, too."

"Ooooh, look at the lotions!" Carrie cried. "They've got sun-tan lotion out already. I love to put that stuff on. I close my eyes and pretend—"

"Pretend *what*, Carrie?" both Elfrida and Victoria said, teasingly.

Carrie smiled. "Well, I pretend I'm one of those famous models who's always getting married a lot. And she's doing this sun-tan lotion commercial for TV. And all the cameras are pointing at her and there are all these lights—"

"Oh. Toothpaste," Victoria said, checking her list.

"—And I get to rub this lotion all over me," Carrie went on, "while everyone watches and says, 'Isn't she glamorous' . . ."

"*And* milk of magnesia," Victoria said.

"Is that it?" Elfrida asked.

"No. Then I get to model beachwear," Carrie said.

13

"Carrie . . . Wake up. I was talking to Vicky."

"That's it," Victoria said. "I have everything. But now I have to go to the cleaner's."

"I think I'd better skip the cleaner's," Elfrida said. "I really have to take the dog out. He'll chew the door off if I don't get home."

"I'll go with you," Carrie said.

"Bye, Vicky," Elfrida said. "See you Monday in school."

"Okay," Victoria answered. "But the cleaner's is the best part. Carrie could pretend she owns all the clothes."

"That's right!" Carrie said, but Elfrida pulled on her arm and dragged her away.

# 3
## *Lucky-Duck Lost*

"**H**ey! It's not here!" Victoria grabbed at the pocket of her smock.

"Did you forget something?" her mother asked, unpacking paper bags on the kitchen table. "Let's see . . . toothpaste, shaving cream, milk of magnesia . . ."

"No, no, not that, it's—" Victoria patted the pockets of her jeans and then checked her cuffs. "It's—" she repeated, and peered into the bags she had brought home.

"You've got everything, Vic," her mother said. "The whole list. Wait, where's the rubber cement? Oh. Here. Thanks, honey, you didn't forget a thing. Did you get any change?"

But Victoria hadn't heard. Victoria was frowning.

15

"I *know* I had it this morning when I left the house. I *always* carry it," she mumbled." And I had it in spelling  . . ."

"Victoria, what are you talking about?" her mother asked as she put the box of Brillo under the sink.

"My Lucky-Duck," Victoria said. "I lost my Lucky-Duck!"

"Oh. That."

"I always have it in my pocket! *Mom,*" she wailed. "It's gone!"

"Aww," her mother said sympathetically. "I'm sorry, Vic. You sure you had it?"

"I *always* have it," Victoria said for the third time. "It's *lost!* It's *gone!* Oh, Mom  . . ."

"Well, honey, it was just a little key chain. I'm sure we can find another one just like it. Come on, now. Don't be too upset  . . ."

"Oh, but, Mom, I've had it since my fifth birthday!"

"I know."

"My *fifth!* I've been carrying it with me for four whole years! Almost my whole life practically!"

"Well, but—"

"Grandma gave it to me. Remember? It was hooked onto the ribbon of the present she gave me? I don't even remember what the *present* was, but I've always kept my Lucky-Duck!"

Her mother sighed. "I know. I've pulled that thing out of the washing machine more times—"

"Oh, Mom—"

"—*And* the dryer! One night it woke me up, rattling around in there!"

"My poor little Lucky-Duck!" Victoria moaned.

"Well, tomorrow I'll try to look for one just like it," her mother promised. "But, Vic . . . there's something I wanted to discuss with you—"

But Victoria was shaking her head. "No. Another one wouldn't be the same. I've got to find it—" Suddenly she brightened. "I know what! I'll go back to each place I went—and look all over for it! And on the sidewalk along the way and—"

"Now, Vic, this is kind of important . . ."

"*This* is important, too, Mom," Victoria said. "Let's see. First we went to the grocery store, then the drugstore . . . and I picked up the cleaning last. I'll go back to each place!"

"But, Vicky, I wanted to—" She stopped

when she realized her daughter wasn't listening. "Okay," she said. "Go back and retrace your steps . . . But don't be too disappointed, now, if you don't find it . . . All right?"

Victoria was half out the door.

"It's my Lucky-Duck!" she cried as she ran off. "I've got to find it!"

# 4
## *Lucky-Duck Found*

Tommy Lundgren hadn't felt like going home after school, and so he dawdled. It was spring, and a sunny, warm day, and going home meant helping with the yard and garden and doing his homework. Tommy had brand-new tennis shoes on his feet, a weed in his mouth, a baseball cap with the visor in the back on his head, and he felt dreamy and restless. There was no baseball practice, his best friend, Ralph, was at the dentist, and there really wasn't any place to go but home. He decided to go home, but slowly.

He peered into the window of the sporting goods store on First Avenue. There was a big canvas tent set up in the middle of the floor. It was blue and had see-through plastic windows that you could roll up and an awning on skinny stilts at the entrance.

Tommy smiled. Just the thing for my back yard, he thought. But his birthday had been in February and Christmas was a long way off and they never did sell camping equipment in the winter time, anyway. He sighed. He figured he'd probably never ever get a tent.

Maybe his birth certificate was wrong! Maybe he was really born in May. Next month. Nope. A little voice inside him nagged that there wasn't much chance his birth certificate was wrong.

Tommy moved on to the next store. Hardware. Hardware was boring. He inspected a red barbecue grill with a hood. Jamie loves hardware stores, Tommy thought, picturing his older brother prowling through aisles, picking up one tool, then another. He sighed again. But Jamie's boring, too, Tommy thought. Jamie was always bragging about how hard high school is and how smart you have to be even to *go* to it. Jamie was always whispering about girls to his stupid friend Jerry, and—

Tommy shook his head. His brother Jamie

was not what he wanted to think about on his own time.

A large black crow dropped to the grass next to the curb, almost at Tommy's feet. It looked up at Tommy with its sharp little eyes. Tommy knelt slowly in order to get a better look at it. He peered around to see if anyone was near. No one was.

"Hey, how come you can fly?" Tommy whispered. "Hey. Show me. What makes you guys fly?"

The crow cocked its head and hopped in another direction, poking at the grass with its beak.

"Hopping's okay," Tommy said to the bird. "Anybody can do that. But how about flying?"

The crow found a shiny brass button in the grass and picked it up.

"Hey, don't eat that," Tommy said. A woman and her little boy came out of the hardware store and Tommy stood up quickly. He didn't want to be caught talking to a bird. The crow flew off with the button still in its beak.

Tommy began to whistle, walking along. Jamie had taught him to whistle.

Suddenly, Tommy's eyes lit up. The drug-store. He could even buy something in there with some of the small change that jingled in his pocket—not like the sporting goods store where everything cost about a zillion dollars . . .

Baseball cards! Tommy grinned widely. Maybe with a little luck he could draw a Steve Garvey! Tommy wasn't a Padres fan—he really rooted for the Atlanta Braves—but Steve Garvey was one of his heroes. Tommy played first base for his own team, the Hawks, and he thought Steve Garvey was the best!

He walked confidently into the drugstore and looked around, smelling the drugstore smells. He knew right where the baseball cards were. But on the way he inspected magazines, birthday cards, pencil cases, erasers in the shapes of footballs and Fred Flintstones.

And then, out of the corner of his eye, he spotted something glittering on the floor. He picked it up and studied it.

It was a key chain, a plain old little-ball key chain, but the charm which dangled from it was a white plastic duck with an orange beak. It seemed to grin the way Donald Duck could grin, but this duck wasn't wearing a sailor suit. It was just white with bright eyes and a smiling beak and something written across its wing.

"Lucky-Duck," Tommy read, mouthing the words. "Lucky-Duck. Hey! I found a lucky duck!" He smiled, and stuffed the charm into his pocket. "Maybe I'll get Steve Garvey!"

Now he hurried to the racks of baseball cards and examined their plastic wrappers.

"One of you has Steve Garvey," he murmured. He closed his eyes and ran one finger over the packs. *"You,"* he said and closed his fist over one of them. "You're *it.*" He paid for the cards and ripped them open.

"Come on, Steve. Come on, Steve," he whispered as he flipped through the cards.

"Dale Murphy!" Tommy cried out loud.

Dale Murphy, an outfielder with the Braves, was just as good as Steve Garvey. "Yay!" Tommy said and clutched the card. He walked quickly toward the door.

He stopped once to make sure the card he held actually showed a picture of the great Dale Murphy, and bumped right into someone entering the store.

"Ow!" Tommy said and rubbed his shoulder. Then he recognized his classmate. "Hi, Victoria. Sorry. I didn't see you."

"It's okay," she mumbled, stooping to look under the rack of sunglasses.

"See you, Victoria," Tommy said as he left, but she was heading toward the magazines and didn't answer.

At home, Tommy helped with the yard and garden and did his homework. His brother Jamie didn't arrive until dinner time. He was on the track team.

"Hi, kid," Jamie said, ruffling Tommy's hair. Tommy winced and pulled back. "What's new?"

"I got Dale Murphy," Tommy told him.

"Oh, yeah?" But Jamie didn't appear interested.

"Yeah. Because I found some luck," Tommy said. He hoped he sounded mysterious.

"You found what?" Jamie had picked up a newspaper and was studying the sports page.

"I found some luck," Tommy repeated. "But I can't tell you what it is."

His brother shrugged.

"Don't you want to know?" Tommy asked, disappointed.

"Okay," Jamie sighed. "What?"

"I can't tell you!" Tommy cried, waiting for his brother to beg him.

"Well, okay then, make up your mind," Jamie said. He went back to his paper.

"Well . . ." Tommy said, giving up. "I'll tell you, but you can't tell anyone else. Jamie?"

"What?"

"I said I'll tell you if you promise not to tell anyone else. Okay?"

"Okay, okay," Jamie said, putting down his paper. "What is it I can't tell anyone?"

Tommy peered around, even though he knew that his father was showering and his mother was in the kitchen.

"Okay," he whispered, digging into his pocket. "Check this out." He held up the key chain to show his brother.

"It's a key chain," Jamie said. "So what?"

"Look at what's on it," Tommy said. He jutted his chin forward. "Just *look* at it, will you?"

Jamie looked. "Lucky-Duck?" he said.

"Yep. That's my new luck. I found it. Wait till you see what it brings me. Today I got Dale

Murphy. Tomorrow . . . Who knows what?" He smiled at his brother and took back the charm.

"You're such a dumb kid," Jamie said.

"Yeah, that's how much *you* know," Tommy told him. "I'll tell you what. I'll bet when we play the Wildcats on Saturday, I'll bet I knock home the winning run! That's what I'll bet. And it's all because of"—he put the key chain back in his pocket—"of my Lucky-Duck."

"You're such a dumb kid," Jamie repeated, and went to wash up for dinner.

# 5

*Hawks vs. Wildcats*

Tommy was up early on Saturday, though his game didn't start till noon. He was excited. All night he had slept with the Lucky-Duck key chain under his pillow. He knew, he just knew, that the Hawks would beat the Wildcats and that he, Tommy, would get the winning hit.

The baseball diamond was the one behind Tommy's elementary school. The field looked smaller than it was because it was hemmed in by stores and a big clothing outlet a block long. It seemed to Tommy that there were getting to be more and more buildings in Wakefield and less places to play. But his father said that things always looked smaller the bigger you got.

Tommy showed up at the ball field a half-hour before noon, but Ralph and his dad, their coach, were already there.

"We're going to win," Tommy said, greeting Ralph. "I know it."

He made a fist and tapped the pocket of his uniform, where he'd put his charm.

"Big chance," Ralph said. "The Wildcats haven't lost one game yet."

"It doesn't matter. We're going to win."

"That's the way, Tom," Mr. Buck said. He patted Tommy's shoulder. "That's the attitude we need!"

"Big chance," Ralph repeated and made a face.

"Ralph . . ." his father said.

"Okay, okay," Ralph said. "We're going to win. Tommy's going to win it for us."

"I *am*," Tommy said and smiled.

"Right!" Mr. Buck answered. He went off to dust the bases.

"Hey," Ralph said when his father had left. "Do you know something I don't? Did the Wildcats' pitcher get sick or something? Because if he's sick, maybe we've got a chance . . ."

But Tommy shook his head. "I don't know

if he's sick or not. But what we've got on our side is . . ."

"What?" Ralph asked.

"Can't tell," Tommy said.

"Why?"

"It'd spoil it. I'll wait until after we win and then I'll tell you."

"Come on, Tommy, no secrets," Ralph said. "Remember when we made our fingers bleed with the pin and mixed our blood and swore that we wouldn't keep any secrets? Remember? You have to tell, it's part of the code."

Tommy took a deep breath. Then he let it out.

"Okay," he said firmly. "I'll tell. But it's just between you and me. Not even your father, not even Mike Wickowsky, not even—"

"Okay! I won't tell anyone! What is it?"

But, still, Tommy kept his hand over his pocket. "Jamie laughed at this," he told Ralph. "He doesn't believe it. But I do. Yesterday I got Dale Murphy on a baseball card and I hardly ever even get any Altanta Braves. And ever since, nothing bad has happened to me at *all*. Nothing! And something bad is *al-*

29

*ways* happening to me. Especially with Jamie."

"Hey, Tommy, what are you talking about?" Ralph asked.

"I got luck," Tommy said softly.

"What?"

"I got *luck*. Can't you hear? Luck! I got it."

Ralph wrinkled his nose and smiled.

"Okay . . . Look!" Tommy held out the key chain. "It's just a plain old key chain, but the charm on it is lucky. See?" He touched the duck's wing. "It says right on it, 'Lucky-Duck.' And it is. It's a special charm with special magic and . . ."

"And what?"

"And we're going to win today. And guess who's knocking in the winning run?"

"You?"

"Me."

"Is that really lucky?" Ralph asked. "Let's see it."

He took the charm and peered at it.

"It'll work, Ralph," Tommy said. "You'll see. I've been lucky ever since I got it."

"Well . . ." Ralph frowned. "I don't know, Tommy . . . I mean—even *I* can go one day without anything bad happening . . ."

"And a Dale Murphy baseball card?"

"Well . . ."

"You'll see. You watch."

Tommy's face got longer and longer with each inning. The Wildcats' pitcher was not only healthy, he was having a good day. The Hawks made only two hits in four innings, while the Wildcats scored five times.

In the sixth, Tommy hit a triple. It was the best Hawks hit so far and the team went wild. Especially Mr. Buck. Then the next batter hit a long ball to the outfield and Tommy came sliding into home to score!

But when the game ended, he was near tears. His was the only Hawks run. Tommy swallowed hard and pinched his nose so that no one would see if he cried.

"That was a great hit, Tom," Mr. Buck said, squeezing the back of Tommy's neck with his hand. "You played a great game."

"Thanks, Mr. Buck," Tommy mumbled.

"What's the matter?" Ralph asked. "You were good. The *rest* of us stunk."

"Yeah, I know," Tommy said. "But we lost."

31

"Well, sure we lost. We were supposed to lose. We only stood a chance if the Wildcats' pitcher was sick or something. I told you."

"Yeah . . . but I told *you* we were going to win. And that I was going to knock in the winning run."

"I know," Ralph said. "But I think you were right about the Lucky-Duck. Maybe the team didn't win, but look at that hit you got! You never got a hit like that before!"

"Yeah, but we *lost*," Tommy said. "That's not lucky!"

"But *you* were lucky!" Ralph insisted. "You got a great hit!"

"But it doesn't matter," Tommy said, "because the team lost."

Ralph sighed. "I think that's one lucky duck you got, Tommy. I wish I had it."

"I thought it was," Tommy said, "but it's just a key chain."

"Trade you for it," Ralph said.

"Yeah?"

"Yeah . . ."

"For what?"

Ralph thought. "Dave Winfield," he said finally.

Tommy said, "Well . . ."

"*And* Reggie Jackson."

Tommy bit his upper lip. "Well . . ." he said again.

"*And* . . ."

"And?"

Ralph inhaled. "Steve Garvey."

"*Steve Garvey?*"

Ralph nodded.

"*Steve Garvey?*"

Ralph nodded harder.

Tommy stuck out his hand with the key chain in it. "You got a deal!" he cried happily.

# 6
## *"Come On, Lucky-Duck!"*

"Come on, Ralphie," Mr. Buck said. "Pick up those extra balls. I'll get the bases. Then we'll go home . . ." They were the last ones left at the field.

Ralph walked over to his father and touched his shoulder.

"It's okay. Dad," he said. "It wasn't your fault. They were just too good. We knew that. They haven't lost a game yet. But we're getting better all the time. You're a good coach, Dad . . ."

Mr. Buck smiled. "Well, thanks," he said. "And we are getting better. We'll get 'em next week. Right?"

"Well . . ." Ralph said, "next week it's the Bears. And the Bears have this hitter who can really—"

"Never mind, Ralph," his father sighed.
"Let's go home."

They began to walk slowly, carrying their
equipment.

"Maybe our luck will change, Dad," Ralph
said. He squeezed the key chain in his hand.
"You never know."

"We can use a change of luck," his father
said. "And I can use a shower. How about
you?"

"I can use a new glove," Ralph said. "Mine
is too small, Dad. Remember you bought it for
me back in first grade?"

"A new glove, huh?"

"Yeah . . ."

"Well, I also think you can use a haircut,
kiddo!"

"I can also use one of those self-pitching
things. You know, this machine that pitches
the ball to you so you can practice your hitting?"

Mr. Buck sighed. "I can use a vacation," he
said.

"Me, too, Dad!" Ralph cried. "How about it?
A vacation! What a great idea!"

"It would be nice, Ralph. Your mom wants
to go to the shore this summer. She always did

like the ocean. Me . . . I like the mountains . . ."

"I like the shore," Ralph said. "And the mountains, too. Which one? Or both, Dad? How about both? We could go to the shore for a week and then the mountains for a week—"

"And then to Europe. For skiing." Mr. Buck shook his head. "I'll tell you, Son, I'm not sure we'll be able to do much of anything this year. Business isn't so good."

Ralph was dismayed. "Nothing? Nothing at all, Dad?"

"Well, maybe we could afford a long weekend somewhere. We'll see . . . Don't count it out yet, Son."

Ralph kicked at a stone on the sidewalk. Gee, he thought, no vacation. Boy, this isn't very lucky. But he said, "Don't worry, Dad. I'll bet something turns up."


That night, Ralph hooked the Lucky-Duck key chain through the top buttonhole of his pajamas. He turned out the little lamp next to his bed and rolled over on his back.

"Come on, Lucky-Duck!" he whispered as he held it in his fist. "We could use some good luck. My dad could sure use it, anyway. Even though I've got you, do you think you could work some good magic for my dad? I guess you'd have to work extra hard, but see what you can do, okay?"

In the warmth of his hand, the little white duck grinned his silly grin.

# 7
*One, Four, Eight, Two, Five, Nine*

Ralph kept the key chain hooked to a belt loop on his jeans all week. Most of the time— at school, at baseball practice, at home—he didn't think about it too much. But every now and then, he touched it. And every time he did, he was sure it warmed his fingers.

Toward the end of the week, Tommy Lundgren asked him if he'd had any luck yet.

"Not really," Ralph answered. "Not yet—"

"Well, maybe *you'll* get a big hit in the game on Saturday," Tommy said. "And after that, you can trade the duck for something else. Tell the kids about it first, so they know that's why you got the hit."

Ralph frowned. "Naw," he said. "It's not a hit I want. It's something better than that."

"I know," Tommy said. "But I'm not sure we can beat the Bears."

"It's not that, either," Ralph said. "It's something very extra special."

"Like what?"

"I don't know yet. But when I know, I'll ask the duck to get it for me."

"I asked for us to win last week," Tommy said. "And we didn't."

"But *you* got a hit," Ralph said. "I think it's supposed to be personal. For the one who owns it. I asked it to do some magic for my dad, but I'm not sure it goes past one person."

"What are you going to ask for, then?" Tommy asked.

But Ralph kept shaking his head. "I told you, I don't know yet. But I'll know when I know!"

Friday night, Ralph sat up in his bed in the dark and leaned against the headboard. He touched the duck hooked to his pajamas.

"I'm not going to ask you to make us win the game tomorrow," he said softly. "Or even for me to get a hit. Just remember. I'd like for us to win and I'd like to get a hit, but I don't want to use up your luck on that. So if I get it"—he squeezed the charm—"it doesn't count, okay?" Then he rolled over and went to sleep.

Saturday morning it poured and the game was canceled. Ralph wasn't sure what kind of luck that was.

It was the following week that the idea hit him. And when it did, he wondered why he hadn't thought of it before. The only problem was that Melissa Brabble was with him at the time. Of all people!

Melissa lived on Ralph's block, so sometimes he found himself walking home with her. He had the feeling that she watched for him after school on purpose and would catch up and tag along just to bug him. And he could hardly ever think of the right thing to say to zing Melissa back!

"You just don't get the rule, Ralph," Melissa was saying. "If you remembered the rule, then you could spell it right every time."

Ralph made faces to himself.

"The thing is, you have to know where to

40

put the apostrophe," she went on. "The apostrophe goes where the letter was left out. You missed *didn't*, remember? Because the apostrophe should have gone where the *o* was. For *did not*. See? Contractions are easy if you just remember that!" She grinned at him and he looked away. "I'm just glad you weren't on my team this week," she said. "Anyway, now that I've explained the rule, you won't miss any contractions if you get on my team *again*."

Ralph sighed.

"I can't wait till the summer," Melissa said, swinging her book bag. She waited a moment for Ralph to ask why. When he didn't, she went right on. "We're going to Florida!" she continued, but Ralph just hitched his books up under his arm and walked a little faster. "We're going to Disney World and Marineland and Epcot and everything!" She had to skip to keep up with Ralph now. "And we're taking a plane, too!" she panted.

They passed a newsstand on the corner and Ralph stopped to look at sports magazines. He hoped that Melissa would skip on home by herself. She didn't. She stopped with him.

"What are you looking at?" she asked.

"*Sports Illustrated,*" Ralph answered. He only looked at the cover because the man at the stand got mad if you picked things up and didn't buy them.

"Oh," Melissa said. "My daddy reads that."

Ralph tried to look interested in the magazine cover so Melissa would get bored and go away. And then he saw it.

A blue-lettered sign.

It said *Lottery Tickets Sold Here.*

He gasped out loud.

"What?" Melissa asked. "What is it?"

Ralph was sorry she had heard him.

"Oh, nothing," he said. He put his hand in his pocket, feeling two dollars and some change. He touched the key chain on his belt loop.

"There is," Melissa said, trying to follow his gaze. "There is, too, something. What is it?"

Ralph cleared his throat. "Nothing. I just thought I'd buy a lottery ticket, that's all. Maybe two."

"That's silly," Melissa said. "Lottery tickets. My daddy wouldn't buy those. He says nobody ever wins lotteries."

"People win," Ralph said, turning to her.

"People win all the time. You see it on TV. You see it in the papers. And Mrs. Green next door had a friend who had a cousin whose family won a million dollars!"

"You don't even stand a chance," Melissa said, sounding forty years old. Ralph hated the way Melissa sounded forty years old. "Nobody ever wins those things, Ralph. You'd be stupid to waste good money on something like that."

Ralph touched the Lucky-Duck. He closed his eyes.

This is it, he said inside his head. This is what I've been waiting for. This is what I need your special magic for. We need to win the lottery. We need it real bad. My dad could stop worrying. And we could have a vacation.

"It's just a stupid old waste of good money," Melissa was saying and Ralph opened his eyes.

"No. I'm going to buy two tickets. And one of them will be a winner. I know it, Melissa."

"*How* do you know?" Melissa asked, sticking her face right next to his. "*How,* anyway?"

If Ralph hadn't been so angry, he never would have told her. But he *was* angry. So he did.

"I have a magic charm," he said. "It's something that brings special luck. And I've been waiting for just the right thing to wish for and now I found it. So I'm going to buy lottery tickets and if you don't like it you can just go take a leap off a train, Melissa!"

Melissa backed up and looked at him. Usually she got away with teasing Ralph. He hardly ever answered back.

"What kind of magic charm?" she asked.

"Never mind."

"Show it to me or I won't believe you," she said.

"I don't care if you believe me," he said.

"Show it to me or I'll tell."

"Tell who? Tell what?"

"Anybody. I'll tell. Ralphie Buck believes in magic charms and he thinks he's going to win the lottery with—"

"Okay!" Ralph said. "Just shut up."

"Let's see it," Melissa said, putting down her book bag.

Ralph lifted his shirt, revealing the dangling key chain with the little grinning white duck on it.

"That?" Melissa said. *"That's* your magic charm?"

"That's it," Ralph said.

44

Melissa wasn't quite sure she should sneer just yet. She reached for the duck and peered at it.

"It's just a stupid key chain that says 'Lucky-Duck' on it. What's so magic about that?"

Ralph turned away from her.

"May I have two lottery tickets, please?" he asked the newsstand man.

The man looked at him. "Ain't supposed to sell 'em to kids," he said.

Melissa smiled. Ralph glared at her.

The newsstand man watched them. "Gamblin', you know," he told Ralph.

"I'm not a gambler," Ralph said. "But this is important."

"Oh, poo," Melissa sneered.

Ralph fixed his eyes on the newsstand man. *Please,* he tried to say with his eyes. *I won't beg in front of her,* he said with his eyes, *but please!*

The newsstand man tried to hide his smile at Ralph's earnest expression. He looked at Melissa's smug face.

"Well . . ." he said.

Ralph made his voice sound casual. "It's only this one time," he said, and repeated, "Just this one time . . ."

"I believe you, kid," the newsstand man said

very seriously. "Just this one time. I'll buy them for you—as a gift—and you can pay me back."

Ralph exhaled loudly with relief and joy. Melissa clucked her tongue and folded her arms.

The newsstand man hid his smile again by ducking his head. "Okay, kid," he said, "what'll it be? You want the instant or the weekly?"

Ralph hesitated.

"The weekly comes out in the paper," the man explained, "You would have to check that. But the instant, that you could find out right away."

Ralph chewed his lip. Not the instant, he thought. I don't want Melissa around when I find out.

"Give me the weekly," Ralph said quickly. He dropped his books onto the counter and gave the man his two dollars. "Two weekly ones."

"Okay. Now you pick six numbers for each." The man handed him a form.

"Six numbers?"

"Any six numbers you want. For each one. Then I send it out, it goes into the computer and you watch the paper."

Ralph gritted his teeth.

"I'll help you pick," Melissa said cheerfully. "How about seven first? My favorite number is seven. On my seventh birthday I got seven dolls. They were all from other countries, one from France, one from Spain, one from—"

Ralph put his hands over his ears. "Melissa, would you just shut up and let me think?" he cried and Melissa looked at the newsstand man and shut up.

"Okay," Ralph said. "One, four, eight . . . two, five, *nine*. That's it for the first one. One, four, eight, two, five, nine."

"Those are no good," Melissa said. "It's too perfect. It's all in order—one, *two,* four, *five,* eight, *nine*. See? You have to mix them up if you're going to win."

"I thought you said *nobody* wins lotteries, Melissa," Ralph said.

"Well," she smirked, "not *that* way."

"Come on, kid, do the next one," the man said. "I haven't got all day."

"All right," Ralph said. "This time I pick six . . . three . . . one . . . two, one again . . . *seven.*"

"Good," Melissa said. "Seven is good."

47

Ralph glared at her.

"You got it, kid." The man took Ralph's name and address. Ralph stood still there at the newsstand and touched the Lucky-Duck again.

You heard it, he said silently to the duck. You heard the numbers. And that's my wish.

He swallowed and grabbed his books. He walked the rest of the way home with Melissa but he didn't hear another word she said.

# 8
## *Lucky Wednesday*

Ralph thought it would be impossible to hold his breath for five days, but he nearly did it. He thought his week was rather lucky, because he didn't see Melissa Brabble at all, except in school, and she never mentioned the lottery tickets. He decided she had probably forgotten about it because she had so many other things to think about, like Disney World and Epcot. So he forgot about Melissa and waited for the day the winning numbers would appear in the paper.

When the day came—Wednesday—Ralph didn't buy the paper on the way home. He knew his father would bring one, and after waiting so long, Ralph decided he wanted to stretch out the excitement just a little longer.

He tried not to grab the paper from his father's hand as soon as he walked in the door. He played a little game with himself. He said hello to his father, never taking his eyes from the rolled-up newspaper. He told his father about his day, and asked about his father's. It was when Mr. Buck tossed the paper on the couch and went to wash up that Ralph could no longer hold himself back.

His heart was beating wildly, but the time was perfect now. He was alone with the paper in his living room.

He didn't need to get his tickets. They were safely hidden in his drawer. He knew the numbers by heart. He had said them to himself for five whole days.

He opened the paper slowly and slowly turned each page until he found the lottery listing.

Licking his lips, he ran his finger down the column of numbers until he found one that began with a one or a six.

And he saw it.

148259.

148259.

ONE FOUR EIGHT TWO FIVE NINE!

His first number, the one Melissa said

wouldn't win because it was too perfect! The Lucky-Duck did it! The Lucky-Duck came through!

And then Ralph let himself scream out loud. His parents came running from the kitchen.

"How much, Ralphie, *how much?*" Tommy cried the next day when Ralph told him.

"Five thousand dollars," Ralph said. "Not a million, but five thousand! You should have seen my dad's face. And my mom's. My mom cried."

"Boy, I'll bet," Tommy said. And then he said, "Boy!"

"I told you I had to wait for just the right thing, didn't I?" Ralph said. "Didn't I? And then I wished so hard. I wished *so* hard!"

"Boy," Tommy repeated, shaking his head. "Nobody you know ever wins those things! That's really something, Ralph, that's really lucky."

"Yeah, that's what Melissa said. 'Nobody ever wins those things.' Wait'll I show her."

"Gee," Tommy said. "All I got was a lousy triple."

# 9
## *Stomachache*

"I don't believe you," Melissa said.

"Well, just go look in last night's paper, then," Ralph said. "Remember the number you told me was too perfect? Just go look, Melissa. I told you the charm is magic!"

But Melissa just stood there with her mouth open. For once, she didn't have anything to say.

"And we're getting our picture taken," Ralph added. "By the newspaper. Because we're a local Wakefield family, they said. So go take your too-perfect numbers, Melissa, and stuff 'em!"

Melissa shrugged and Ralph walked away.

She stared after him a long time, frowning.

She bit her lip and moved her left foot around in a circle.

Then she made up her mind.

When Class 4-B had gym, Melissa made believe she had a stomachache. She got excused from class, and when she was sure no one was watching, she slipped into the boys' locker room. Quickly she went through each locker until she found Ralph's jeans with the Lucky-Duck charm hanging from the belt loop.

I'll just borrow it, Melissa said to herself. Just for a little while. I'll get it back to him somehow. But for now, I'll just . . . borrow it.

She opened the door a crack. No one was around. She could hear the sounds of her classmates doing acrobatics in the gym. Quickly she left the locker room and hurried down the hall toward the nurse's office to lie down and rest her stomach.

The nurse put Melissa on a green cot opposite her desk in her office. It wasn't very private. Kids kept streaming in and out, and the nurse felt foreheads, took temperatures and handed out bandages. But Melissa didn't mind. She turned toward a wall, clutched the Lucky-Duck in her fist and made wish after wish. Finally, she fell asleep, smiling.

She woke up a half-hour later, startled. Then she remembered where she was and why she was there. The nurse peered at her over her desk.

"Feeling better, Melissa?" the nurse asked.

"Oh, much!" Melissa answered, sitting up. "Much better."

"Good. I guess you really needed some sleep. What time do you go to bed in the evening, dear?"

"Nine," Melissa answered quickly. It was true that her bedtime was nine, but sometimes she turned on the TV in her room—very softly, so no one would hear—and watched until she fell asleep. Sometimes the TV was still on when Melissa's radio-alarm went off in the morning.

"Well . . . Do you want to go back to your class now?" the nurse asked.

"Yes. I'm fine now." Melissa slipped the key chain into her sports sock. "Thank you," she added, as she left the office.


The class was in the middle of social studies when Melissa got back. Mrs. Berry nodded at her.

"Feel better, dear?"

"Yes, thank you," Melissa said and took her seat.

She looked over at Ralph. His chin was resting on his fist. He looked as if the last thing in the world he was thinking about was famous explorers.

Mrs. Berry had asked a question and hands were being raised around Melissa.

"Elfrida?" Mrs. Berry called.

"1497!" Elfrida answered.

"1498!" someone else called out and Elfrida turned in her seat.

"No," Elfrida said, "It was 1497. That was the first voyage. In the second one—that was 1498—*that's* when he got to Greenland and sailed on to Chesapeake Bay."

"Who?" Melissa whispered to the girl next to her.

"John Cabot," the girl answered. "Sh!"

Melissa leaned back and touched her sock. The charm had slid down to the top of her shoe. She tried to flatten the sock so the Lucky-Duck wouldn't bulge, while opening her social studies book to the "John Cabot" part. She looked over the page quickly and rubbed her ankle.

"And what is the main thing we remember about John Cabot?" Mrs. Berry asked. "Victoria?"

"That he was born Giovanni Caboto in Italy but he worked for Henry the Seventh?"

"No-oo . . . Ralph?"

"Yes, Mrs. Berry?"

"Have you been listening, Ralph?" Mrs. Berry asked.

"Uh-huh . . ."

"Well? . . . What makes John Cabot's voyages memorable to us?" she repeated.

Ralph said, "Uh . . ."

"Ralph, are you all right?" Mrs. Berry asked. "You look a little pale."

"Aw, I'm okay," Ralph said. "But I guess my attention isn't the greatest right now, Mrs. Berry . . ."

"I see . . ."

Melissa waved her hand frantically and Mrs. Berry called on her.

"John Cabot's discoveries served as the basis for English claims in North America!" Melissa said loudly. She had just read it.

"Very good. Now, let's talk about Francis Drake."

Melissa leaned over to Ralph.

"What's the matter?" she asked. She was sure she knew. She was sure Ralph had discovered his Lucky-Duck was gone. But she wanted to double-check.

Ralph sighed. He didn't answer her.

"What's the *matter?*" Melissa repeated and the girl in front of her said, "Sh!"

"Nothing," Ralph said. He opened his social studies book.

"There is *too,*" Melissa insisted and the girl in front scowled at her.

Ralph turned quickly in his seat. "It's none of your business!" he growled at Melissa.

Mrs. Berry said, "Ralph, another outburst like that and I'm sending a note home to your parents!"

Melissa hoped Ralph was upset about something besides the Lucky-Duck, so she could feel a little better about having taken it. Her conscience bothered her . . . but not that much.

# 10
## *Important Wishes*

Ralph and Tommy walked toward a slide at the end of the playground. Ralph sat down and leaned backwards against the cool metal. Tommy sat at his feet in the dirt hole made by hundreds of children over the years as they got to the end of their ride.

"I know it was on my belt loop when we went into gym," Ralph said.

"You sure? It could have dropped off in the hall, you know. That happens with those key chains sometimes. They just come un-hooked—you never even realize it. It just dropped off, Ralphie, that's all . . ."

Ralph sat up. "Well," he said, "I guess I shouldn't complain. I waited for a good wish, I made a good wish and I got my good wish. So that's it, right?"

Tommy looked at his friend. "You know what I think?" he asked. He didn't wait for an answer. "I think . . . that the Lucky-Duck works one time. For one person. And then it disappears. That's part of its magic. Now someone else probably has it—just like I found it on the drugstore floor—and whoever that is will have a good hunk of luck, too. And then it'll move on to someone else. What do you think, Ralph?"

"Well—"

"Because it's like you're not supposed to have too much of a good thing, you know? Just once. Just once to let you know there's magic around, then *poof!*" He snapped his fingers. "Gone. Don't you think so?"

"I—"

"I'll bet there's someone right now who's looking down at the floor in school and saying, 'Hey! What's that? It's a Lucky-Duck, that's what it is!' And then that person will do just what I did and just what you did and make a special wish and it'll come true and then you know what will happen?"

"I guess—"

"Right! It'll disappear on 'em. And move on to someone else."

"Gee—"

"That's how magic works, Ralph. That's how it works. Every time."

Tommy clapped Ralph on the shoulder and they both stood and walked toward the back of the school for afternoon baseball practice.

Melissa crept out from behind a bush near the slide. She had followed both boys to hear what they might say about the Lucky-Duck and she heard just what she needed to know. What if Tommy were right? She began thinking. You got your wish and you lost the duck . . .

She had planned to return the charm to Ralph—she really had, she told herself—but maybe someone else was supposed to get it after all. Maybe that was the way magic worked, as Tommy said.

She smiled to herself. Passing on magic. That was a neat idea. Of course, she had pushed a little for her turn at it . . .

But now for the wish! Melissa was reaching down to take the charm out of her sock when a voice above her made her jump.

"Melissa? What are you doing here? School's been over for nearly an hour!"

Melissa stood up quickly, cleared her throat and faced Victoria Hansen.

"Hi, Vicky—" she said. "I'm not doing any-thing—just . . . hanging around for a while . . . What are *you* doing here?"

Victoria sat on the slide. "Nothing. I'm just looking, that's all. I'm looking at the school I won't be going to any more, and at the play-ground I won't be playing at any more and—"

"Wait a second. What do you mean?" Mel-issa asked.

"Oh, I found out we have to move," Victo-ria said, digging her toe into the dirt hole. "I've really known about it for a week now, but the closer we get to the end of school the worse I feel . . ."

Victoria bit her upper lip.

"I keep wandering around," she said. "I keep looking at things. Stores . . . We're not even gone yet, and I even miss *you*, Melissa!"

"Where are you moving to?" Melissa asked. She wished Victoria would move *now*.

"I don't know . . . There are two jobs in two different places and my father doesn't know which one he's taking, but it doesn't make any difference because what we have to do is *move!* And I like it here in Wakefield."

"Well, gee, that's tough," Melissa said.

"Yeah! What I could use is a miracle," Victoria said. "A genie in a bottle, like Aladdin had. Remember that story? I could use a real miracle. I'll bet this never even would have happened if I hadn't—"

"What?" Melissa asked.

"Nothing." Victoria had been about to say, ". . . if I hadn't lost my Lucky-Duck," but she couldn't say that to Melissa Brabble, who would think she was crazy. Lucky-Duck had been Victoria's secret since she was five! She shook her head and said, "Nothing," again.

Melissa's lips twitched. Victoria could probably use this Lucky-Duck, she thought. Probably I should give it back to Ralph after I get my own wish . . . But maybe I'll give it to Victoria instead . . .

If . . . she thought, looking away from Victoria, *if* I don't have any other important wishes coming up that will make me want to hang onto it . . .

Victoria stood. "I'm going over to look at my old kindergarten room," she said with a sigh. "I had such happy days there . . ."

"Bye," Melissa said. She had other things on her mind and she began to walk home slowly.

I always wanted a real fur coat, she thought to herself. Mommy has a Persian lamb coat and it's *so* soft and curly and sweet . . .

But fur is awful hot in the summer. Maybe I'll wait until September to wish for that.

I'd like a long black car . . . and a chauffeur to drive me to school every day. And wait for me outside to take me home.

Melissa smiled a big smile at the thought of climbing into her long black car.

And there'll be a TV in it. And a video-game machine. And a refrigerator and a freezer for ice cream! Oh, boy, that's Wish Number One. She closed her eyes and bent down to take the Lucky-Duck out of her sock. It was beginning to hurt her ankle.

Holding the charm in her hand, Melissa wished. First: a long, black, shiny car with a chauffeur and electronic games and a TV and a refrigerator and a freezer! And right away, she added in her thoughts.

She began to skip toward home. I'll wait until I get there, she said to herself, to think of the rest!

# 11
*More Important Wishes*

When Melissa got home that afternoon, she found Mary Lee there. Mary Lee came in to clean and take care of Melissa's five-year-old brother, Pooky, whenever Melissa's mother wasn't home. Mary Lee was a high-school senior. She got home from school at one-thirty and could spend the afternoon and evening if she were needed. She often was needed at Melissa's house.

Mary Lee smiled. "Hi, Meliss."

"Where's my mother?" Melissa grumped back at her.

"She's shopping, I think. Or at a meeting. Maybe both. Aren't you glad to see me?"

Melissa shrugged.

"How was school?"

"All right. I had a stomachache and I had to lie down in the nurse's office."

"Ohh . ." Mary Lee felt Melissa's forehead. Melissa pulled away.

"I don't have a *temp*-era-ture," she said. "I just had a stomachache. I think I'd better lie down some more." She wanted to be alone in her room.

"I was going to take Pooky over to the park," Mary Lee said, "and I thought maybe you'd come with us . . . But if you're really not feeling well, I guess we'll stay here."

"No, it's okay. You can go without me. I'll just go upstairs."

"I think we'd better stay," Mary Lee said. "I'll play in the back yard with Pooky. If you need me, that's where I'll be."

"Okay . . ."

Melissa climbed the stairs, went into her room and closed the door.

She sat down on her pink carpet and stared at the pink flowered wallpaper and the pink bed with the canopy over it.

"All right," she said, clutching the Lucky-Duck. "I told you about the car and chauffeur. What I'd like is to have it parked in the driveway by . . . by . . ." She frowned. Better give it a little time, she thought.

". . . by morning. When I wake up in the morning. And then . . . I'd like a drawer full of brand-new summer shirts. These are the colors I want: powder blue, white, maroon, orange, navy, light green and dark green and . . . a few striped ones. Okay? And bathing suits. I need a *lot* of bathing suits, especially since we're going to Florida. Make them all the same colors as the shirts except . . . I want *two* powder blue ones. But different styles." She blew on the charm for extra luck. "And then . . ."

There was a knock on her door.

"Melis? You okay?" It was Mary Lee.

"Yes!" Melissa cried, afraid anyone butting in would spoil the magic. "Go away!"

"Hey, watch it," Mary Lee said. "I'm only trying to help. Want me to see if I can get in touch with your mom? Or dad?"

"No! No, I'm fine, Mary Lee, really. Thank you," she added. "I'm sorry I yelled. I was thinking."

"Thinking, huh?"

"Yes!"

"Need help thinking?"

"No . . ."

"Can I come in, Meliss?" Pooky called from outside the door.

Melissa heard Mary Lee say, "No, Pook, not now. Your sister's thinking. She needs all the quiet she can get!"

Melissa waited until the sound of their footsteps died away.

Then she closed her eyes tighter than ever and grasped the charm until it dug into her palm.

"Where was I? Bathing suits. Right. And I would like . . ." She breathed in. "This one will be hard . . . I would like a zillion dollars! A zillion! That's a lot more than a million or a billion. Because then I'd have to pay a lot of taxes, the way daddy always says when he throws pencils at the wall. But a zillion—nobody could even count that high, I bet!"

She shook the charm between her two cupped hands.

"You hear? A car. A chauffeur. Shirts. Bathing suits. A zillion dollars. And what else can I think of . . .?

She kicked her heels into the carpet.

"What else? Oh! I'd like a playhouse. Not like that one—" She looked over at the doll's house she had gotten for Christmas. It was four feet high and stood against one wall. "I mean a *real* one, that I can walk in. With electricity. And a real telephone. And a stove and a sink that has real water. And speaking of that, a bathroom, too. And also a television! One in the car and one in the playhouse."

Suddenly, she felt tired. All that wishing! She flopped back onto the carpet and slid off her shoes. She could hear Pooky's happy laugh from the back yard as he and Mary Lee threw a ball back and forth. Someday, she thought, they'll have to start calling him Patrick or he'll be sorry. One day he'll be middle-aged and president of some big corporation and his vice-president will come in and say, "We're having a board meeting, Pooky!"

Melissa chuckled to herself at the thought of that. And my children will call him "Uncle Pooky"! Yuck! How awful! Uncle Pooky. I'll start calling him Patrick *now* and start taking care of his whole future life!

She sat up. I will go to the park, she thought, feeling better.

She went over to the window.

"Mary Lee!" she called down. "I changed my mind. I'd like to go the the park after all! With you . . . and *Patrick!*"

She paused in her bounce down the stairs.

"Don't forget!" she said out loud. "Two powder blue bathing suits, but *two different styles!*"

# 12
## *Is There Magic?*

The park was crowded. There were lots of
toddlers with their parents or baby sitters. Dog
walkers strolled and some groups of girls
jumped rope. It was a small park, but there
weren't too many open spaces in Wakefield so
the park was the place most people thought
of visiting on a nice day.

Melissa knew two of the girls in the jump-
rope game but she didn't feel like joining them
right away. She sat down on a bench to watch.
Mary Lee and Pooky went to the swings.

Melissa's mind began to wander. Besides
clothes, there were some other things she
wanted . . . A charm bracelet with tiny gold
charms that did things—maybe a little car with
wheels that really turned, and a teeny heart

that opened up . . . and maybe a pussycat with jewels for eyes—

"Oh!" She jumped, startled, as something furry brushed against her legs.

"Hi!" Elfrida Rapp called to her. "Sorry he scared you. He loves people!" With a grin, she reached down and picked up her dog, Risky, who was crouched under Melissa's bench. "Naughty, Risk!" she said, tugging softly on his ear. "You scared Melissa."

"You should keep him on a leash," Melissa declared. Her heart was still beating rapidly. "He could run into traffic or something."

"In the park? Naw . . ." Elfrida sat down next to her. "What are you doing, Melissa? Just sitting?"

"Uh-huh."

"I just saw Pooky and Mary Lee. Gee, he's really getting big, isn't he?"

*"Patrick,"* Melissa said.

"Patrick?"

"I decided he couldn't go through middle age with a name like Pooky."

"He's not *that* big," Elfrida said, looking across at the swings.

"Oh, you know what I mean. *Pooky's* so silly . . ."

"Well, look at *my* name. *Elfrida* isn't exactly what you picture walking down a runway with a bouquet and a crown.

Melissa laughed. "Well, yeah, but *Elfrida* isn't silly. It's just weird."

"I know. My father had a weird sense of humor. He's the one who picked it. He told me it was because it was different—"

"*Mmm*, it's different, all right . . ."

". . . and because it sounded prankish."

"Prankish?"

"You know, impish. He always called me Elf."

"All the kids call you Elf," Melissa said.

"I know. I like it. Maybe because it was my father's idea. Sometimes I wonder what he would've named his other kids if he'd had any."

Melissa stretched. "Probably not *Pooky*," she said. "Elfrida, do you believe in magic?"

Elfrida looked up quickly. She noticed that talking about her father since he died made other kids nervous. They usually changed the subject. "You mean like at your birthday party last month?" she asked. "Where the magician pulled a rabbit out of a hat?"

"No—"

Elfrida laughed. "I liked when he pulled the mouse out from behind your cousin Ruthie's ear! Boy, did she scream!"

"Not *that* kind of magic—"

"And the trick with the cards? That was *neat*, Melissa! Did you ever ask him how he did that one? He guessed *every single*—"

"I don't *mean* magician magic, Elfrida, " Melissa interrupted. "I mean *real* magic. Not tricks. *Real* magic."

"What do you mean, *real* magic?"

"Oh, like . . . fairy godmothers or something."

"Fairy *godmothers?*" Elfrida began to giggle.

"Never mind," Melissa sighed.

But Elfrida was still enjoying it. "You mean like—spit on your palm, knock your elbows together, stamp each foot twice, say 'Abracadabra Mesopotamia' and knock on wood? That kind of magic?"

Melissa didn't answer.

"No, I guess not," Elfrida said. "I guess I don't believe in magic. I liked *E.T.*, though . . . Did you?"

"Did I what?"

"Like *E.T.?*"

"Oh. I guess so . . ."

"Me, too. I loved that they could ride bicycles up in the sky. That looked like fun. But I don't believe you could *really* ride bicycles up in the sky . . . if that's the kind of magic you mean."

"That's it," Melissa said.

"*Carrie* would believe in that, I bet," Elfrida said. "Carrie is always pretending. Sometimes her pretends are off-the-wall! But she's so nice . . . it doesn't make me mad or anything."

"Like what?" Melissa asked. "What does Carrie pretend?"

"What? Oh, let's see . . . Well, one of her favorites is that she's a famous child movie star. One time she put on lots of her mother's makeup—you know, like Mrs. Berry does? She tried to copy Mrs. Berry's green eyelids, only she got some on her ears, too. Anyway, she put on all this makeup and then she put up her hair . . ."

"How?"

"Oh, you know, like this—" Elfrida pulled her own hair up and wound curls around her finger that hung over her forehead and into her eyes. "And she walked like this—" She stood and tiptoed around the park bench, causing a boy in a Budweiser T-shirt to toss her a funny look. Elfrida giggled, let down her hair and sat again. "And I was supposed to tell her which way to move . . . and look at the camera . . . and all that. She was funny. But she loves that pretend best . . . being a movie star. Carrie does."

Melissa smiled.

"Well . . . I'd better get Risky home," Elfrida said, reaching down to clip the dog's leash on his collar. "Did you do your social studies report yet, Melissa?"

But Melissa was staring straight ahead.

"Hey, Melissa? Did you do that report yet? On explorers?"

Melissa nodded, still staring. Elfrida shrugged.

"See you in school," Elfrida said as she moved away, but Melissa didn't answer. She hadn't heard her. She was thinking.

A movie star! I hadn't even *thought* about that! Wouldn't everyone just die if I turned out to be a famous wonderful movie star! *That's* what I want, she thought, hitting her fist against her palm. I'll even give up some of the shirts. And take only *one* powder blue bathing suit. A movie star! That's the best! She smiled so widely that Pooky and Mary Lee waved happily at her, glad to see her change of mood.

# 13
*Nobody Knows*

Melissa woke up early the following morning, even before her radio-alarm had a chance to go off: something that *never* happened.

She jumped up quickly, ran to her window, then to her closet, then to her bureau. She climbed back into bed, flopped back against the pillows and counted all the discoveries she'd made in the thirty seconds she'd been up.

One—there wasn't *any* car in her driveway, not a long one, not a black one, not *any* one. Even her father's very own car wasn't there. And her mother's station wagon was probably in the garage.

Two—there wasn't a single new shirt in any of her bureau drawers. Not one. Every one of

the shirts she saw was left over from last year.
Last year!

Three—there wasn't one bathing suit anywhere. Not new or old. Not even on top of
her closet shelf. Instead of having a whole new
wardrobe of bathing suits, she was absolutely
bathing-suitless! Altogether!

Four—she definitely had not received a zillion dollars. Having shaken her piggy bank
quickly, she knew that there still remained exactly six dollars and twenty-three cents in
change, just what had been there yesterday,
the day before and last week. There was nothing hidden under her socks or her shirts or
her shorts. No zillion dollars. No checks. No
IOU's.

Five—there was no beautiful charm bracelet
in her jewelry box. There was a seashell neck-
lace, a mother-of-pearl bracelet and a tiny
birthstone ring she'd gotten as a baby. There
were two marbles, four buttons and a glass pin
in the shape of a parrot—everything that had
been there for years and years and *years!*

And six—six was worst of all—she was pretty
positive she wasn't a movie star. If she had
been, the phone would have been ringing off

its hook by now. Someone would have brought in a gorgeous tray with her breakfast on it, not to mention a small vase with flowers to top it off. And surely *someone* would have come in to help her choose her clothes and put on her makeup for the day's shooting! None of these things had happened and she was sure she was still just plain Melissa Brabble of Class 4-B at Wakefield Elementary who hadn't even bothered to do her homework the night before because she'd been sure she wouldn't need it in the morning!

*"Grrrrrrr,"* Melissa growled, just as her radio-alarm went off with the same sound. She slammed the off button with her fist. What rotten luck, she thought. What stupid, terrible, rotten, rotten *luck!*

Luck . . .

She went back to her bureau. There it was, that dumb key chain, hanging over the ear of her china dog. She'd truly forgotten about its being the source of all her dreams and wishes coming true. Now, she decided, it was the source of all the bad luck she was having! She snatched it off the dog's ear and glowered at it.

Stupid, dumb key chain. Lucky-Duck! Some magic. Some luck! Now she'd have to do her homework in about twenty minutes in order to get to school on time and not be yelled at in the bargain!

"*Oooooooh*," she said angrily through puckered lips as she pulled on a pair of tan-colored jeans. "I'm going to get rid of this stupid thing . . . Just *looking* at it makes me feel embarrassed! Lucky-Duck . . ."

The duck grinned its orange-beaky grin at her. "*Ooooh*," she said again, stuffing it into her pocket. "Am I glad I didn't *tell* anyone about this! To think, I nearly told Elfrida yesterday!"

She shuddered, then leaned against the wall with relief. But I didn't, she thought. I never said anything. That's the only luck I *did* get. Nobody knows what I nutso I was! A dumb, stupid key chain . . . Oh, Melissa, you *nerdiest* of nerds!

But it's okay. Nobody knows.

She pulled on one of last year's shirts.

"I am going to throw this thing so *far*," she said out loud, her voice muffled by the shirt, "that I won't ever have to look at it again!"

Then she raced downstairs to put together a three-page report on Coronado.

The report took longer than she had thought it would and Melissa was late. She blamed it on the Lucky-Duck and ground her teeth together as she hurried down the street, cutting across lawns.

"I'm late and my report is just terrible and I didn't get one thing I wished for and it's all your *fault!*" she said, smacking her fist against her pocket where she had put the charm. "I'm going to get rid of you *now!*" She stopped next to a big tree in someone's back yard, pulled out the Lucky-Duck and glared at it. "The only good thing about today is that it's *Friday!*" she shouted.

A woman poked her head out of a window in the house behind Melissa.

"What are you doing on my lawn?" the woman yelled.

"Uh—nothing—" Melissa said, embarrassed. "I just cut through on my way to—"

"Don't be trampling my lawn!" the woman hollered, waving her arm.

"I'm going!" Melissa called and whispered to the Lucky-Duck, "And so are you!" She pulled her arm back as far as she could and threw the charm into some nearby bushes.

"Good riddance!" she cried, then hurried out of the yard. She had forgotten all about her silent promise to return the Lucky-Duck to Ralph.

# 14
## *A Shortcut*

An almost summery week went by for Wakefield and Class 4-B. The children and even Mrs. Berry kept looking toward the open windows, anxious to be out enjoying the weather. Tommy Lundgren and Ralph Buck went to baseball practice, traded baseball cards and talked about the vacations they would be taking with their families once school was out. They never mentioned the Lucky-Duck to each other—not once, though each boy thought about it from time to time and smiled in secret to himself.

Victoria Hansen sighed a lot. She felt sure that this move her family was planning would never have come up if she had managed to hold on to the special charm that she'd had since her fifth birthday—"almost my whole life practically!" as she said.

Melissa Brabble never thought about the Lucky-Duck at all.

It was Monday morning. Elfrida Rapp was under her bed.

"Elf! Where are you?" her mother called.

"Here!" Elfrida called back.

"Where's 'here'?"

"Under my bed!"

"Oh, sure," her mother said. "I should have thought of that." She came down the hall and into Elfrida's bedroom. "Elf?" she said.

"In a second . . ."

Mrs. Rapp listened to her daughter scraping around under the bed. She put her fingers to her lips to keep from smiling, then asked, "What's the big attraction down there?"

"Some of my science project. It's due today," Elfrida answered. She crawled out, holding two large photographs. "I don't know how they got there . . . but it's a good thing I checked. I'm still missing one."

"You mean those pictures you took of your plants? Aw, Elf, I thought you had all those in that nice booklet you made . . ."

"Well, I did, once . . . But I took them out a couple of times and I changed a few . . . Anyway, some of them got lost."

"Well, I think you'd better get going," her mother said. "Did you walk Risky?"

"Uh-huh . . . Before you got up."

"Oh. Good. Well, I'm off to work," her mother said and kissed her. "Good luck with your report."

"Thanks," Elfrida said. She put her pictures together and slipped them into their cover. Then she gathered her books and walked downstairs.

Risky was at the front door. He sniffed Elfrida's shoes.

"Can't pet you, Risk," Elfrida said, "My arms are too full . . ." She managed to get the door open, but as she did, the little dog raced out of the house and across the front yard.

"Oh, rats!" Elfrida cried, putting her books down on the stoop. "Risky! Get back here, Risky!"

But the dog bounded ahead and scooted

under the neighbors' bushes, where he began to dig.

"Risky! Don't dig in the Grubers' bushes! You know how fussy they are about their lawn and plants . . ." She reached under a bush, but she couldn't catch the dog. Suddenly, she heard and felt a rip. The sleeve of her blouse had caught on a thorn.

"Oh, rats, Risky, I don't have time to change. Come out here!"

The dog's little face appeared from under a bush.

"Gotcha!" Elfrida cried and grabbed his collar. He turned his face away from her and something fell from his mouth. He struggled to get it back.

"What's that, Risky? What've you found?" Elfrida reached for it. "Aww," she said, "it's a little key chain. But it's not good for dogs to chew on."

Her skirt had no pockets, so she clipped the key chain to her wraparound sash.

"Thanks, Risky. That's a nice present. Now you get back in the house!" She put him inside, closed the door and grabbed all her books and pictures. Then she began to run.

The school was four blocks away and Elfrida decided to take a shortcut through a vacant lot with woods at the end of it.

She had to duck under some low branches and that's when she heard the ripping sound again. The tear in her sleeve that had begun in the Grubers' bushes had caught on a branch and from the sound and the sudden breeze on her back, Elfrida knew her blouse was a goner. Sure enough, when she stood up, the blouse was hanging in tatters off her shoulder.

Elfrida put her books down and sat on them.

"This day is not starting out very well," she said aloud.

She tapped her foot.

"I can't go anywhere with no blouse on," she said, frowning.

She looked around. There wasn't a soul in sight. Only trees. And bushes.

"Well," she said, getting up, "a bush ripped my shirt, so a bush is going to have to supply me with a new one."

It took a while, but she managed, pulling and wrapping until she had covered the top half of her body with branches and leaves and roots. The leaves tickled, but it would have to do as a shirt until she got to school and borrowed something from the lost-and-found.

"Elf!"

"Hey, look at Elf!"

Science class was already in progress when Elfrida walked in, wearing her bush.

"Elfrida Rapp, is that you?" Mrs. Berry asked, blinking her long-lashed eyelids.

She could see the bangs and braids, but the rest of Elfrida seemed to be all sticks and leaves and books.

"Sorry I'm late," Elfrida said. "Can I go to the lost-and-found?"

The kids were standing at their desks now, staring at Elfrida.

"Boy," Tommy breathed. "What a neat science project!"

"Elf always thinks of the best things!" Carrie cried. "Dressing up as a tree! Wow!"

"That's really good," another girl said. "Gee, all I did was take pictures of plants!"

Elfrida put her books down on her desk.

She adjusted the branches that were scratching and tickling. "Uh . . ." she said.

"Well, Elfrida, it certainly is a unique idea," Mrs . Berry said, nodding. "Fred has just finished the solar system. Why don't you explain your project now."

Elfrida looked at Mrs. Berry. She looked at the class.

"Come on, Elf!" Victoria called.

Elfrida said, "Okay . . " She pulled at a leaf under her arm. "Well, Mrs. Berry, you said the purpose of this project was to get closer to nature . . ."

# 15
## Among Friends

Elfrida sat quietly while her classmates gave their own science reports. She had to sit quietly or some part of what she was wearing would scratch or tickle her. At least she felt cool in her tree-blouse. The weather was still unusually warm.

During one boy's report on dandelions, Mrs. Berry opened another window.

"How's that? Better?" she asked the class and they all nodded, relieved by the slight breeze. Elfrida sniffed the air. The boy went back to his dandelion report.

*Bzzzzzzzz-zz-z.*

Most of the class barely noticed, but Elfrida lifted her eyelids. She was right next to the open window and she heard it.

*Bz-zz-zz-zzzzzzz-z.*

90

The source of the buzz was in the room now, swirling somewhere over Elfrida's head. She couldn't squirm in her seat because the quieter she sat, the less she itched.

"Did you hear that?" she whispered to Carrie.

"What?" Carrie whispered back.

"Never mind," Elfrida said as Mrs. Berry looked at her.

*Bz.*

Then she saw it. It was some sort of bee. Elfrida felt she should know what kind because they had studied insects in science. But she didn't know what kind. All she knew was that there was a bee in the room and it was somewhere near her.

*BZZZZZZZZZ-ZZZ-z.*

It landed. It landed right on one of Elfrida's shoulder branches. Moving only her eyeballs, Elfrida stared at the bee. It was happily buzzing and moving among the leaves.

"Go away," Elfrida whispered out of the corner of her mouth.

"What?" Carrie asked.

"Not you," Elfrida said. "Bee."

"What?"

"Bee!" Elfrida answered.

"Elfrida Rapp," Mrs. Berry said, "you've given your report. Please give the others the same attention they gave you."

"Sorry, Mrs. Berry," Elfrida said, "but there's a—"

"Later, Elfrida, please."

"Okay . . ."

The bee moved on to another leaf. Elfrida followed it with her eyes.

*Bzzz-zz.*

Tommy's desk was in front of Elfrida's. He heard the sound and turned around in his seat. He followed Elfrida's crossed eyes and saw the hovering insect.

"A BEEEEEEEEEEEEE-EE!" Tommy screamed. Mrs. Berry dropped her pencil. The boy with the dandelions dropped them in a floating bouquet. The class jumped.

"OW!" Elfrida yelled as the bee stung her wrist. "OW! OW!"

"It was a bee, Mrs. Berry," Tommy explained. "Elf had a bee on her."

"I see," Mrs. Berry said, patting her chest and clearing her throat. "Well. Elfrida, you'd better go to the nurse and have that sting looked at."

Elfrida, sucking at her wrist and blinking tears from her eyes, nodded and stood up.

"Listen, Tommy," she said as she moved past him, "if you ever see a bee on me again, *don't yell!*"

The nurse helped Elfrida unbranch. Then she cleaned her scratches and tended the bee sting.

"That was quite a science project, Elfrida," the nurse said.

"Yes," Elfrida agreed, "it was."

"Did Mrs. Berry like it?"

Elfrida gingerly touched her wrist. "Uh-huh," she said. "I got a bee. I got a bee in science." She laughed at herself.

The nurse laughed, too. Then she said, "Well, now what about your own shirt? The one you wore to school. The one without twigs."

"It ripped," Elfrida explained. "I was going to see if I could borrow one from the lost-and-found."

"Oh. Well, why don't I get one for you?" the nurse said. "I'll just pull a screen around the cot and you wait here."

No sooner had she left than Carrie tiptoed into the office.

"Elf?" she called softly.

"In here." Elfrida peeked out from behind the screen around her cot.

"Are you okay? Did your whole arm swell up and everything?"

"No. I'm fine," Elfrida told her, holding up her wrist. "See?"

"I got stung by a bee once," Carrie said. "Right here." She touched her cheek. "My whole face swelled up like a balloon. My brother called me Bubblehead for a month. Gee, that was a good science report, Elf! I thought you were doing plant pictures."

Elfrida laughed. "I *was!* This was an accident. I tore my shirt on the way to school and wore the branches till I could get to the lost-and-found."

"Really?"

"Really."

"Well, it sure turned out okay. Mrs. Berry is still talking about how creative you were. Say, what's that?" She was looking at the wraparound sash of Elfrida's skirt.

"Oh. That. It's a present from Risky. He brought it to me to say he was sorry for running away this morning." She unhooked the

94

key chain from her skirt and handed it to Carrie.

"Oooh, it's a good-luck charm," Carrie said. "It says 'Lucky-Duck' on it."

"Ha! Some good-luck charm," Elfrida said. "I got stung by a bee."

"Yes, but look how your science project turned out! You never would have gotten so much praise for plant pictures. Three kids did that."

"Hello, Carrie," the nurse said, coming back into the office. "Did you want to see me?"

"Uh—no, I just wanted to see how Elf was feeling."

"Well, she's fine. And now she has a shirt, too. I had an awful time finding something for you, Elfrida . . ."

"Aw, I don't care about the size," Elfrida said.

"No, I was just trying to find something *clean*," the nurse told her. "But here's a fairly decent T-shirt. . ." She held it out and Elfrida put it on.

"Here's your Lucky-Duck back," Carrie said as they began to walk to their class. "You better hang on to it. Who knows what your next project will be?"

"Oh, that's silly, Carrie. It wasn't any good-luck charm. I just thought fast, that's all."

"*I* believe in good-luck charms," Carrie said.

"You do?"

"Uh-huh. And spells and witches and enchantment and—"

"Okay, Carrie, okay—" Elfrida said, cutting her off with a laugh. "You can have it." She handed her the Lucky-Duck. "You keep it."

"No kidding?"

"No kidding. It's all yours."

Carrie took it tenderly. "Oooh," she breathed. "Thanks, Elfrida. You're the best friend I ever had . . ."

# 16
*Lucky-Duck Moves On. And Up.*

Carrie spent the rest of the afternoon dreaming. She hardly heard the explanation of mixed numbers. She barely caught the rule about doubling consonants. She missed the social studies chapter on Eric the Red entirely.

Carrie was thinking about magic. And witchcraft. And spells. And charms.

Charms.

As soon as school was out, she raced to the library. She would have told Elfrida why she was going, but she knew that her good friend would only smile.

So she went alone to the shelf that contained books about warlocks and witches, elves, leprechauns, demons. Clutching the Lucky-Duck in her fist as she turned pages, she murmured to herself.

"I know it's magic," she said. "Lucky-Duck. A lucky find. It worked for Elfrida even though she didn't know it. And it'll work better for me because I *do* know it."

She pored over the books.

And in one, she found what she was looking for.

"Spells to Make You Beautiful" was the title of the chapter.

"Oh, I'd love to be beautiful," Carrie sighed to herself. "If I were beautiful I'd be such a big star . . . Or Miss America . . . or Miss *Universe!*" She thought about that for fifteen minutes until she remembered where she was. Then she carefully copied one of the spells onto a blank page in her math notebook.

"Where could I buy 'eye of newt'?" she asked herself as she left the library and came out into the bright sunlight of the late afternoon. "What *is* 'eye of newt'? It sounds disgusting, but maybe it's just a kind of medicine . . ."

She stopped and frowned.

Medicine, she thought. You get medicine in the drugstore. Maybe the drugstore sells "eye of newt" and "henbane."

She hooked the Lucky-Duck onto the but-

tonhole in her shirt and began to skip down
Main Street toward the drugstore.

She was in a hurry. She couldn't wait to try
the spell. This was the best pretend of all, she
thought as she skipped. Because this one could
come true . . .

She was in a hurry. So she didn't realize that
the little ball in the silver key chain wasn't
hooked tightly enough in its catch. And she
never felt it break apart and slip to the sidewalk because she was lost in her dreams. And
she was in a hurry.

"Hi, Carrie!"

"Oh, hi, Victoria! Back in the drugstore
again, huh?"

"Yep. We keep running out of toothpaste.
What are you doing here? Pretending again?"

Carrie grinned. "Uh-huh. But this time it's a
good one! I have a special charm and I'm
going to buy some things to make a real magic
spell!"

"Let's see the charm," Victoria said. "What
is it?"

Carrie looked down at her shirt. She gasped.

"It's gone!" she cried. "Oh, Vicky, it must
have fallen off!"

"Well . . ." Victoria said, "don't feel bad. I lost a lucky charm, too, and I was sure that's why we were going to have to move. But guess what?"

"What?"

"We're not moving! My dad got a raise and he's not going to take a new job somewhere else after all!"

"Oh, Vicky, I'm so glad!" Carrie cried.

"Me, too! And I never did find that charm so I guess it had nothing to do with good luck or bad luck after all . . ."

Carrie sighed. "Well," she said, "I sure wish I'd had the chance to find out for myself. Elfrida gave me that charm and I was sure it would be lucky for me . . ."

"Elfrida doesn't believe in charms," Victoria said, smiling.

"I know. That's why she gave it to me."

"Where'd she get it?" Victoria asked.

"Her dog found it."

"Really?" Victoria said. "What kind of charm was it, anyway?"


Tommy Lundgren, running down Main Street to see how fast his still-new sneakers could carry him, almost collided with Melissa on her twelve-speed Panasonic.

"Oh, Tommy, you could have wrecked my bike!" she cried, before pedaling away.

Tommy was staring after her when a black crow walked boldly up to him from the grass near the curb and began to pull at his shoelaces.

"Hey!" Tommy grinned, looking down. "You the same guy I met before?"

The crow looked up, then hopped away.

"Bet you are," Tommy said. "Hi, there, Crow. How you doing?"

The crow cocked his head.

"Me, too," Tommy said, and continued on his way.


The crow moved on along the edge of the curb. Something glittery caught his eye.

"Aha!" he cawed. "Aha!" He hopped over and picked up the shiny key chain with the little white duck hanging from it. The duck did not interest him. It was the shiny metal chain that did.

Off he flew, high above Main Street, high above the yards and houses of the people who lived in Wakefield, past the woods and the town park and over the baseball field to one of the windows of the elementary school, where he landed.

It was near this window, in a large tree, that the crow had a nest. His mate watched him sail up to the nest's edge.

"Aha!" she cawed, as he dropped the Lucky-Duck next to three shiny metal buttons, two paper clips, a gold circle pin, a mashed piece of foil and a locket on a chain.

A good haul.

Mrs. Berry, working at her desk, shook her head at the cawing outside her window and went on correcting papers.